JU

Mr. Putter and Tabby
Bake the Cake

CYNTHIA RYLANT

Mr. Putter and Tabby Bake the Cake

Illustrated by

ARTHUR HOWARD

Harcourt Brace & Company

San Diego   New York   London

For Allyn, Dave, and Zuma Jay Johnston
—C. R.

To Ray, Laurence, Andrea, Kathleen,
and Robert Gray
—A. H.

Text copyright © 1994 by Cynthia Rylant
Illustrations copyright © 1994 by Arthur Howard

Requests for permission to make
copies of any part of the work should be mailed to:
Permissions Department, Harcourt Brace & Company,
6277 Sea Harbor Drive,
Orlando, Florida 32887-6777.

Library of Congress Cataloging-in-Publication
Data is available upon request.
ISBN 0-15-200205-7
ISBN 0-15-200214-6 (pbk.)

Printed in Singapore

First edition
A B C D E

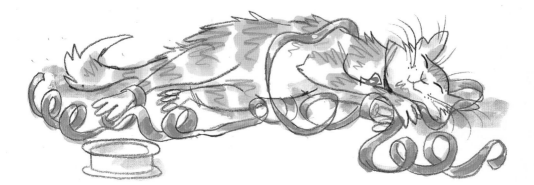

1

A Good Cake

It was wintertime.

Mr. Putter and his fine cat, Tabby,

sat at their window every night

to watch the snow come down.

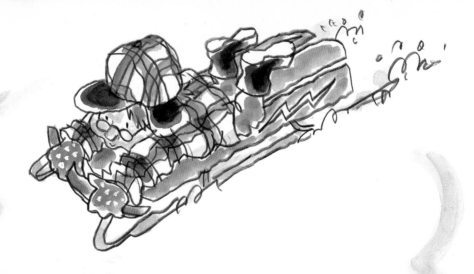

They watched and dreamed.
Mr. Putter dreamed of the
big red sled he rode as a boy.
He dreamed of snowmen
big as a house.

Tabby dreamed, too.
She dreamed of the snowdrifts
she walked on as a kitten.
She dreamed of deep tunnels
through white yards.

Mr. Putter and Tabby were old now.

They had a lot to dream about.

That is why they loved wintertime.

They also loved wintertime because
wintertime brought Christmas.

Mr. Putter loved to give
Christmas presents.
He started thinking about
Christmas presents in July.
He liked to think of what
he could give to the grocer,
and to the librarian,
and to the postman.

Mr. Putter also had to think
of what he could give to his
neighbor Mrs. Teaberry.
This was hardest of all.
He usually had to think about this
all the way to December.

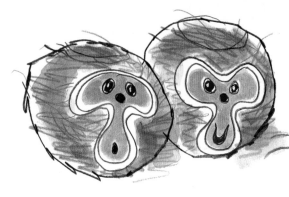

Mrs. Teaberry liked strange things.
She liked coconuts made into
monkey heads.
She liked salt shakers that walked
across the table.
She liked little dresses for her teapots.
She even liked fruitcake.

Mr. Putter could live with monkey heads
and walking salt shakers
and dressed-up teapots.

But Mr. Putter could not believe
that Mrs. Teaberry liked fruitcake.
He could not believe that *anyone*
liked fruitcake.

Every Christmas Mrs. Teaberry

ate mounds of fruitcake.

It worried Mr. Putter.

This winter it was worrying him a lot.

He thought Mrs. Teaberry should have
a good cake for Christmas.
Not a fruitcake that could break her toe
if she dropped it.
A good cake. A light and airy cake.

And one night as he and Tabby
sat dreaming at their snowy window,
that is what he decided to give
Mrs. Teaberry for Christmas.
Mr. Putter would bake her
a Christmas cake.

It would be a cinch.

2

No Pans

The cake was not a cinch.
In the first place,
Mr. Putter did not know how to
bake a cake.
He could bake instant muffins.
He could bake instant popovers.
But he had never baked a cake.
He didn't know how.

In the second place,
Mr. Putter had no pans.
He had muffin pans.
He had popover pans.
But he had no cake pans.

If he baked a cake,
it would have to be
in a shoe.

Or maybe in a flowerpot.

Or even in a hat.

But not in a cake pan,
because he did not have one.

And in the third place,
Mr. Putter had no cookbook.
He had books on seaweed.
He had books on clouds.
He had books on
Chinese trees.
But he had no
cookbooks.

Mr. Putter thought about

no cookbooks,

no cake pans,

and the fact that

he did not bake cakes.

He said to Tabby,

"Maybe for Christmas

Mrs. Teaberry would like

a nice cup of tea and a card."

3

Mary Sue

One week before Christmas,
Mr. Putter and Tabby
took a trip to The Sweet Shop.
It was owned by a woman
famous for her cakes.

She baked cakes with names like
Strawberry Watermelon Pumpkin Apple
Brownie Surprise.

Her name was Mary Sue,
and if anyone could teach
Mr. Putter to bake a cake, it would be she.
Mr. Putter told her his story.

He wanted to bake a
Christmas cake, he said.
Something light.
Something airy.
Something that
would not break
a person's toe.
Mary Sue listened carefully.
She took good notes.
And then she began
to sell him things.

She sold Mr. Putter
seven bowls.
She sold Mr. Putter
three sifters.
She sold Mr. Putter
ten spoons,
five cups,
two spatulas,
a roll of waxed paper,
and a Christmas tree pan.
Then she sold him an
Easy Baker cookbook
and sent him out the door.

Mr. Putter had spent
one hundred dollars.
And he still didn't have any flour.

4

Something Airy

On Christmas Eve

Mr. Putter had everything he needed.

He had flour, sugar, eggs.

He had spoons, bowls, sifters.

He had a cookbook.

He had a pan.

And he had a good cat to keep

him company.

Mr. Putter baked all night long.
His first cake fell flat.

His second cake
wouldn't leave the pan.

His third cake
caught on fire.

By the time he baked his fourth cake,
it was Christmas morning.
Mr. Putter's eyes were droopy.
His face was saggy.
He was moving very slowly.

But Mr. Putter did not give up.
And by nine o'clock in the morning,
he had made the most
beautiful Christmas cake
in the whole world.
It was light.
It was airy.
It would not break a person's toe.

He woke up Tabby,
and together they took the cake
to Mrs. Teaberry.

Mrs. Teaberry was delighted!

She was thrilled!

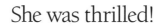

She was PATIENT.

Because as soon
as Mr. Putter sat down
in her chair,
he fell asleep.

And she had to wait twelve hours
before she could cut her cake.
She wouldn't have any without
Mr. Putter, and that is
how long he slept.

But when he finally woke up,

Mrs. Teaberry was there with Tabby

and her own dog, Zeke,

and they ate cake

and drank tea

and watched the snow fall

all night long.

And Mr. Putter and Tabby went home with
a very nice toaster
that sang "America the Beautiful"
when the bread popped up.

The illustrations in this book were done in pencil, watercolor,
gouache, and Sennelier pastels on 90-pound vellum paper.
The display type was set in Artcraft by Harcourt Brace & Company
Photocomposition Center, San Diego, California.
The text type was set in Berkeley Old Style Book
by Thompson Type, San Diego, California.
Color separations were made by Bright Arts, Ltd., Singapore.
Printed and bound by Tien Wah Press, Singapore
This book was printed with soya-based inks on Leykam recycled
paper, which contains more than 20 percent postconsumer waste
and has a total recycled content of at least 50 percent.
Production supervision by Warren Wallerstein and Ginger Boyer
Designed by Arthur Howard and Carolyn Stafford-Griffin